Snowbird

A Spiritual Woman's Journey Through A Traumatic Brain Injury

ELSIBETH HOYT

ISBN 978-1-953223-90-6 (paperback)
ISBN 978-1-953223-91-3 (digital)

Rushmore Press LLC
1 800 460 9188
www.rushmorepress.com

Printed in the United States of America

Chapter 1

A traumatic brain injury left me feeling not myself and out of touch with this world. My fuse was quicker, and my crying and frustration bred anger within the people closest to me who were only trying to be by my side. I used to be an outgoing, social individual before the head injury, but after, I withdrew from society. My friends didn't understand me after the head injury, and I didn't know myself. The hit to my skull, among other things, had dislodged home. Before the accident, everyone respected me. I was physically active and successful in my community and family.

The people closest to me went through nearly as much as I did. They needed to grieve in their own way. In some ways it was a trial for them. I knew their grieving process would be a long one, and I opted to have patience with them because their support would be paramount to my recovery. The injury a person sustained had shaken so many things loose that they started to forget things. My domestic life fell by the wayside and forgot to play with my kids, I forgot to pick up the groceries; I even forgot how to love my kid. My husband asked me why I needed so much support. Then proceeded to inform me to let him support me so I could be stronger within myself. Everyone's story is different, but support from loved ones is a universal need for the injured self.

Being a normal and happy teenager hit a brick wall while snowboarding on spring break in 2006. My home life was ideal. I grew up in a home where I was loved and supported in all I did. After high school graduation came, I chose to move from my home in Salem to Redmond when my father got a job there. I attended college in

Bend where I would pursue my two dreams of government work and competing in the Miss USA Pageant Organization. Understanding the person that I was before the accident is vital to recognize the scope of my injury.

I was always an outgoing and a sweet kid, an optimist who always aspired to make the world a better place. I went to church with my family. My faith was that God's purpose for me in life was to show the love in his heart for the world by being the fun and friendly person he made me. It might seem paradoxical for a roof to mean freedom, but for me, that's what the roof of my church was. I would always gaze up at the ceiling. Its beautiful wood and stained-glass windows brought daydreams of what life might be like when I grew up. You could boil the church down to a gathering of the faithful, but that's not all it is. For me, it was singing, songs, it was love and being loved, and it was...it was just a happy place.

My childhood was a good one. I enjoyed being a little girl and dressing up my Barbies and taking them on safaris in our backyard jungle. As I got older, I would play Monopoly with my brother. Our backyard was spacious. My brother, my sister and I once dug a big hole big enough to fit all three of us, and so it became a fort. There was a school behind our yard, and every Saturday I would ask my dad for some money to buy candy and to play on the playground. My childhood was full of magic. My bicycle was a motorcycle, and dressed up with my sister and neighborhood friends, it became our royal court. I always played the groom on account of my height at that age, but still, I loved to play outside.

I was always the social butterfly and never wanted for a friend by my side. Growing up in the Simi Valley of California my best friend taught me lessons that have stuck with me always. She taught me to enjoy life with another person, with neighborhood plays, school field trips, sleepovers, and seeing what life is like from another family's perspective. We grew up and shared many memories. She had the personality of a true leader. I looked up to her. I remember her father telling me one day, "My daughter looks up to you Elsibeth, so take charge and she will follow." My friendships were an outlet for me to discover my true self.

A few years later I met a girl that lived near me. Over the coming years, she and I would create many memories. We would talk and wash the neighbor's ice blue corvette. She taught me to enjoy life. We would go to the park and play on the monkey bars and pretend the sand was hot lava.

Grade school was a challenge for me. I went to an advanced fundamental school in Southern California. I got Bs and Cs. The principal told my mom I was an average student and that was all I would ever be.

That would turn out to be not quite true later in my school years. I liked school: asking questions in class, writing creative papers, learning histories like the California Gold Rush, the stories of Native Americans, and the early American missions. Field trips were my favorite. There was whale watching where I saw dolphins clustered in formation and a California mission where I got to dress in native wear. School was both social and academic, providing an opportunity for me to express and be myself.

Call it childhood naivety, but I did not realize how fortunate I was to travel the country growing up. My family lived a few hours from Disneyland, so the trips were often, and my favorite ride was Small World. What I enjoyed most was seeing the children from all over the world. The Timber Splash ride and all the princesses were wondrous. As I got older, I went to Magic Mountain, and because of my size, I rode the roller coaster younger than most. Sometimes, height has its perks. I even enjoyed the Viper and Freefall which were scary but thrilling.

Every other year, my family would drive up to Washington and go to Christian family camp for a week. Camp had everything. There was a lake and a blob (a floatation device you would jump into on the lake from a high dive), boating, fishing, a huge tire swing, family campfires, devotionals, and plenty of other families to meet. In fifth grade, we took a vacation to Hawaii with my aunt and uncle who lived there. I got to experience a luau and dance the hula on stage in real life. The ocean was warm, and my life was full of love. The next year, my family went on a road trip from Southern California to Calgary, Alberta. We stopped at state parks; my favorite of which were Custer's Last Stand and Bryce Canyon. I was privileged and blessed that my parents sacrificed so much to provide us with these experiences.

I remember the rush of emotions when my parents told me that we were moving to Oregon. I was about to be in sixth grade. What about my friends and my school and the theme parks I loved so much? Regardless, in the summer before sixth grade, my family moved to Salem, Oregon. In time, I planted my heart in Salem and it grew there. During the last days of that summer just before school, my sister and brother explored the city. Naturally, I had all the jitters incumbent upon a middle-school girl. What will I wear? What friends will I meet? Will I be cool? What I didn't know was that the dearest friend I've had in my life was waiting just outside the school. I was trying to open the door to my new school though it had a sign that said, "out of order." She kindly informed me of this, and we laughed. Opening the other door, we walked together in middle school through every moment and memory. We had the same first class and sat next to each other. I flourished academically. Due to my rigorous grade school training I was able to pull straight As throughout middle school. My yearbook read that I was known as sweet, kind, and friendly from almost everyone. People thought I was older because of my height. I had green eyes and blonde hair. I was never teased or bullied in middle school. I was blessed to be affirmed with burgeoning outer and inner beauty at such a young age.

Class projects and friendships were the highlights of my middle school years. I would dress up for history projects, and I even participated in choir and sang many special songs. A few days later, I would meet another close friend. She invited me to a church group at her house, and over many years, their family became dear friends. Her family encouraged and inspired me to continue in my faith as a teenager. Because of them I became more involved in church loving to sing and learn about the Bible. Seventh grade was one of the most formative years of my life. I was figuring out who and what I was going to be—what friends I would follow, what thoughts and daydreams would fill my mind, and what style and things I would use to define myself. I struggled, but in the end, I found peace in true friends and enjoying my life as I always had.

High school were the years where I developed an internal strength. For me, that meant a vow of abstinence from the trappings of adolescent life. In my freshman year, I enjoyed the roar of the crowd during autumn football games. I danced and went to various church activities. My life was full and happy. On sophomore year, I joined the debate team where I memorized eight-minute speeches on controversial topics such creationism versus evolution and group debates.

People encouraged me to model, and I was eventually scouted by an agency and modeling school at the state fair. At sixteen, I was accepted by the John Casablanca Modeling School. After school, I was in a book called "Teen Dream Jobs." I would model in the Portland Bridal Show and every so often I would do runway shows. I played tennis on junior varsity.

I continued in choir and competed in state competitions where our school won first place. I sang on my worship team in church throughout high school. This was an outlet for me to love both myself and other people. I excelled with my voice and had small dreams of fame in high school, so I pursued the love of singing and sharing my voice with others later in college.

Chapter 2

High school was a time of becoming closer with my younger sister. We went to church functions and school functions together. Around the same time, in 2002, my brother joined the Marine Corps. And so, the boy I knew transformed into a man before my eyes. During boot camp, we wrote letters, and he became ever more conscientious of his family and appreciated his parents more than ever.

My mom shared her love of riding horses with me and worked various jobs to help support the family. I enjoyed our horses, riding them about once a week in middle school and high school. My father was a fun man and worked hard through job layoffs to always find a way to support his family.

To make a point, I will leave out the names of my greater family. It was not as individuals that they helped me through the head trauma, but as parts of a greater whole. My family inspired me in many ways. They motivated me to keep moving forward in my life, even if the topic of my head injury was only mentioned rarely. My only living grandparent passed in 2003. I was blessed to have known my grandpa. It was easy to see from whom my father had picked up his good nature. His soul was filled to the brim with life and song. He was a man who taught me how to fish, cook, appreciate classical music, and value education. These two were not the only positive male role models in my life.

My mom's brothers are tall and strong men. They experienced life in an honest sort of way and shared their wisdom with me. My aunt and uncle supported us kids in school and came to choir concerts. Yet another aunt and her daughter opened my eyes to a love for style, love for life, and appreciation for pageant competitions which is how I chose to embrace my femininity. Together, we enjoyed the family cabin. One of my aunties and I share the same birthday. Our souls are cut from the same cloth. We are both sweet and kind people with a servant heart. When I was young, I would meet up for cabin camp at the family cabin in Sandy where we would have school, make crafts, have fun, dress up, and share the young memories that would eventually light our older years. The year 1995 brought about the loss of both my grandmothers, but as I remember, they were strong, independent women that loved their family and God.

After junior year, I was accepted into a prestigious summer program at Georgetown University called "The Junior Statesmen of America." I raised $3,000 in my community from service organizations and my family and friends. During the summer program, I earned college credit for constitutional law. I debated the morality of the death penalty. I heard Colin Powell and Justice Scalia speak. I met people from all over America, and it was here that I was my true self. When I returned to school, I chartered a Junior Statesmen at my high school and became school president. I produced a fashion show to raise money for Junior Statesmen of America where I had fifteen models and raised several hundred dollars. My transition from childhood to adulthood had finally begun in earnest.

I traveled with the choir to Canada in my sophomore year and to New York City in my senior year. I was able to meet with agencies Ford, Elite, and Trump. They all praised my portfolio and looks as commercial and pretty but not as exotic. Though I had a love for it, I decided to not pursue modeling but college and a potential career in government.

I believe that God directed me to go to college. I had never been to Bend before, and I thought the scenery was just as beautiful as the people. When I prayed just a quiet little prayer on campus, I knew that college was the right decision. My heart was filled with joy, peace, and a passion for the area. After I got accepted, I interviewed, and was chosen for a position on campus as a general council member to the associated students of the college which is equivalent to student government in high school.

My freshman year was near the best of my life. I claimed honors in college for my academics, participated in the college jazz choir, and enjoyed many experiences in student government. I organized a campus-wide political debate during the 2004 elections. In February, I hosted a tax workshop, created a spring fling barbeque and concert, and organized a comedy show from Los Angeles. I learned clerical and administrative skills, how to work a budget, and how to manage meetings. The student life director was a mentor who talked and encouraged me often. My professional life was beginning to take shape alongside my emerging adulthood.

That same year, I participated in Miss Oregon USA as Miss Redmond. I spent a whole year getting physically fit, saving for outfits, and providing community service to build awareness of the prevention of methamphetamine with Central Oregon youth. I met with the sheriff, local elementary schools, and service clubs. The day of the pageant I was ready to win. My figure was in top shape and my mind alert and ready for the challenge. I ended the competition with fourth runner up out of thirty young ladies. I was honored to receive that placing and treasure the experience still.

In 2005, I got a chance to put all the lessons of charity I had learned at church into practice. Katrina sunk New Orleans without prejudice or a shred of mercy. I knew I had to help, and so I raised $12,000 with a team of twelve from the community college in Bend. With that, we were sent to the disaster area. In some ways, it was the trip of a lifetime. But I'll never forget the devastation and destruction that I witnessed there. We spent three days gutting just a single house—twelve of us and one house. It was hard not to feel like a single drop in a very big ocean. We stayed at a church and watched Fantastic Four one evening and ate southern comfort food. Despite the apparent ending of their world, these people still had the time to treat us with humanity. With simple acts of kindness in all that chaos, I was taught the strength of the human spirit.

Chapter 3

After Katrina and back in Bend, I made a decision that would change my life forever. I have always had an adventurous spirit and I've always craved a challenge. To try something new, I registered for a snowboarding class in college. I was there every Sunday with instruction in the morning and free snowboard time in the afternoon to practice what I learned. I even got pretty good. At that time, helmets were not required by the school class at the college. Perhaps if they were, things may have been different.

On the day of my accident, my uncle and his friend invited me to snowboard and ski on Mt. Hood. It was a rare icy spring day, and frozen droplets dripped from branches of trees like crystal chandeliers. My parents told me not to go, and they were right to. With no helmet, I hit the summit and fell at the bottom of the mile run. A rough estimate had me going at a speed of about 35 miles per hour. It was a hard fall, and I blacked out for three minutes. When I woke up, I saw stars like a cartoon. By the time my uncle and his friend found me, I was down, but no one knew how much I had changed or how my life would change or how blessed I was. No one knew I had survived a traumatic brain injury. I returned home in my car, making the two-hour drive from Mt. Hood to Redmond. No one knew I needed physical treatment and analysis—analysis which would not occur for another six weeks. My doctor, although a wonderful doctor, was out of town for four weeks.

Living through the next morning was all it took for me to know I had changed. I was in a constant state of confusion, I was impulsive, and I could not concentrate on anything. I started to display behavior that concerned the people surrounding me. At school, I was always punctual and an active listener and learner. Just days after the accident, a lifetime of good habits were undone. I got to class late, I didn't have assignments done, and I wouldn't participate. I remember a class where I was learning political thought. I was trying to read a book on complex philosophical thought, my focus would wax and wane. One day, the margins were too full, and the other I couldn't make out a single sentence. I was not stable nor strong as I had usually been. Socially, I felt paranoid like everyone was watching me; the implied pressure became too momentous for me to function normally. I would impulsively walk in confused geometry throughout the school property in straight lines and repeated steps. There was no thought behind these actions, but it was clear that they had become imperative. I felt dizzy, frustrated, and confused. I had no way to correct these problems. I tried to even enjoy my jazz class, and it was hard to concentrate on singing a whole song through without getting antsy.

My church was within walking distance from my school. A few days after my accident, I walked to the church on a weekday. I had developed relationships with pastors and staff. My filter, however, was completely destroyed. I walked in on meetings just to say hi. I talked to people I normally did not. I asked for a ride back to the college. A lady pastor gave me a ride and met my mom telling her what was going on. Even the pastor knew that something had gone wrong, she just didn't know what it was. My mom did not know the extent of the accident at this time. The church, over the years, tried being supportive, but instead only alienated me in the process. The love and acceptance I had once found there seemed to have been misplaced.

My family was aware that after I had spent the day with my uncle and that I hit my head on ice. But since I drove home safe and was capable of functioning on the surface, there was no cause to think something had gone seriously wrong. So, we decided to make an appointment with our family doctor when she came home from vacation within the month.

My parents were doing what they thought was in the best interest of their daughter. They weren't bad people, just misinformed.

I had no physical pain, flashbacks, or outbursts of emotion. But I internalized more than I used to. There were no signs of my head trauma right after the accident except those odd behaviors. Over the years, this has been hard for me to comprehend because I would have rather left in an ambulance the day of the accident and gotten checked and diagnosed. You see, the ambulance is only scary for as long as the ride to the doctor takes. But the horror of the weeks that were to follow me in the months of uncertainty and second guessing, I would not wish on anyone. I looked fine but inside I had changed. My life was, all of a sudden, a challenge. I felt alienated, lost, and confused. I wondered if I would ever come back to the person I used to be.

At school, I couldn't concentrate on a single task at hand. My job in the student life center was beginning to be too much. I would bring in more projects than I could handle. One of the staff noticed and asked if I was okay, telling me that I seemed different. Another staff member talked to me, and I had explained my accident earlier. Being self-motivated, I wanted to sustain the same workload I previously had so I shrugged off their concern. These two were concerned that I had not been to the doctor since my fall. They told me they wanted to take me for a car ride. It was vague, but I had no reason not to trust them. Where they actually took me was to the emergency room at the hospital and persuaded me to get checked. I did not leave that hospital for nearly a month.

The hospital is sometimes a blur for me. I don't know a lot about what went on because I spent much of this time outside of my own body, or at least it felt that way.

I do not remember much of the hospital. But suddenly, I had to explain my accident and get treatment. I barely recall being in the hospital in the beginning. There were layers of medical staff that assisted me as a head injury patient. First was a physical doctor who is responsible for body sickness such as headaches after a TBI (traumatic brain injury) or nausea. Second, there is a nurse who looks at behavior and the practical effects or your medicine. Then, a social worker who dissects your life: your idiosyncrasies, your job, your relationships, and your social security benefits. Finally, a psychiatrist figures out the best medication for your brain and checks in with how it is functioning day to day. I had a hard time explaining myself to all these professionals because I had been surviving on my own for over three weeks and had no personal knowledge of head injuries or the language with which these professionals communicated about them. I felt as though I had been thrown to the wolves with no one to understand me and no one to trust.

Chapter 4

The purpose of my story is to help other people honestly without hurting anyone who was trying to help in the process. My first doctor at the hospital was overwhelmed with the information I gave him. The doctor then referred me to a social worker so the staff could find an appropriate placement for me in the healthcare system. Across from the hospital was a competitive but expensive therapy center. Perhaps things might have been different had I been sent there sooner. But things being how they are, red tape kept me from my eventual destination. Finally, they sent me across the street.

My parents were contacted that evening. One of the most emotional confused times in my life was when my dad came to visit me. I saw him talking to the doctor through the clear glass sliding doors in the emergency room. He looked concerned in a desperate sort of way. The same way a tiger looks behind bars at the zoo. The look you have when the will to fight is there but the opportunity is absent.

He was allowed with my permission to come into the room. I was agitated and scared. I felt betrayed at my lack of treatment, but I told him I did not want to go home. I did not feel safe leaving the hospital until I knew if I was all right. It wasn't that Mom and Dad were advocating for a complete lack of treatment. My parents just wanted to wait to see my regular doctor to make sure I had the best care possible. It was important to them that I see a doctor who knew me before the head injury, one who could vouch for my normality and one who knew my behavior day to day. But such discussions are not for the injured.

Wounded, my primary concern was normalcy. I wanted to stop crying, I wanted to eat again, sleep again, and I wanted to go to my job. Caring for someone can be the most painful experience of your life. I'm willing to bet anyone would tell you the same. Love can make you irrational, as it did to my parents. I understand that they only wanted the best for me, but in the process, they risked my immediate medical care. So, we paced around our cages like zoo tigers.

Things happen for a reason. I don't know why I was tricked into being left at the hospital with people who cared but really did not know me or my family or even yet my condition. I don't know why apart from being hurt and confused in the moment that I directed my distrust towards my family at my stay in the hospital. There were no rooms the first few nights at the therapy center, so I was sent within the hospital to a safe location where I had a room. Without insurance and no assurance or results back on any MRI or testing of the brain, I was sent to the mental ward. As stated in California law, you stay in the main hospital to be treated with a traumatic brain injury not psychiatric.

I did not cry, get depressed, and I wasn't even happy. I wasn't anything at all. I went into functioning mode. As soon as I was moved from the emergency room, the social worker advocated for my departure to the therapy center as soon as possible. She was pretty and caring. She checked on me three times. I think she wanted me so much to feel safe. She French braided my hair, and it calmed me and helped me feel comfortable in an uncomfortable situation. She felt much like a guardian angel to me during those low times. Life, though, isn't a storybook. Later, I found that she was talking about me behind my back at a nail salon in town where I got my nails done for my pageant career. She was releasing private records from the hospital concerning me, which is illegal, but more importantly hurtful to me.

When I got close to the mental ward my gut told me "buck up." I walked in and received a bar of soap, a toothbrush, toothpaste, lotion, a hairbrush, shampoo, a towel and my "prison blues" of hospital pants and shirt. There was a room with all glass were the staff running this ward stayed monitoring with cameras. A hallway with glass and a lockdown door in place prevented anyone from leaving or entering. In essence, I was on lockdown.

Two things got me through my stay: eating and grooming. It's funny to think about now, but the way I held on to my humanity in that place was by reciting my daily routines from the outside. I survived my stay by eating all my free meals and snacks upon request and by brushing my hair, braiding my hair, brushing my teeth, and washing my face and hair. This kept me calm. The door to my room was open to the hallway with other patients. This wasn't the worst of it. My bathroom adjacent to my room was joined to the other patient's room. The bathroom was cold surgical metal, basic, bad showerhead, and a very basic toilet that had a loud flush and water that more dribbled than ran in the sink. The staff allowed me to lock the bathroom from the other patient upon request. The bedroom wasn't too bad. There was a bed and a large locked window to the outside world which seemed very far away.

I didn't think about what I was going through. I didn't pray. I didn't get happy. I didn't even get depressed. My emotions were stripped away from me like my civilian clothing. My first contact with the other inmates was someone screaming blasphemies through my bedroom wall in the small hours of the morning. Another lady was haggard looking and paced the hallway, occasionally breaking to sit and stare into space. Overtime, I came to align my journey through this mental ward with Ashley Judd's in Double Jeopardy. She had to face prison for a crime she did not commit and embraced her situation into an opportunity to function as normally as possible within a place of no escape. She did not lose her heart to track down her son and retain her self-respect. Likewise, I refused to lose my faith in God and the respect that I carried for myself.

Visitors for patients in the hospital no matter how serious your stay are very special. Two ladies from my church visited me in the mental ward and were allowed in my room. I got books, and they prayed with me and smiled reassuring me that God cared and so did they. My parents visited a couple times. Once I did not want to see them, and I just took the items they brought me to feel at home.

Finally, a room opened up for me at the hospital therapy center. I remember being let out of the locked doors and being escorted to the facility. I was so systemized that when I got to that next step of freedom I froze up when I entered another locked door despite the center's much homier environment. Finally, I got to my room. It was like I stepped into *Beauty and the Beast*. Compared to the mental ward, this therapy center was an enchanted castle. But castles, like prisons, have walls to keep people in and the world out. Just like Belle, I was scared, hungry, nervous, and excited. If the rehabilitation center was the beast's magic castle, my nurse was Madame de Garderobe. She was so sweet and asked if I was okay. She treated me as a person with feelings as opposed to a person needing observation. My bed was soft, the blankets comforted me, and I had oak shelves and a spacious room with a window. This would become my home for almost three weeks.

This physical therapy center was a much better experience. The staff who helped me there was extensive. The doctor, usually psychiatrist and physician doctors, would come in every few days and talk about how the medicine was affecting me and everything in general.

To get released from this therapy center, the doctor must approve of your release. There are nurses there that check vital signs, blood pressure, and dispense meds. The daily living staff are the team that runs the office, gives you your meals, and runs therapy sessions. Therapy sessions were like having several classes a day. There were classes on physical exercise, classes on nutrition, and spirituality. The foremost purpose of these classes was to facilitate emotional vulnerability. The meals were fantastic and there were activities like puzzles and drawing to work on between classes. TV and movies were available, although limited. You were allowed to have personal items like clothes, iPod, books, and such. The other patients' reasons for being there were diverse. I tried hard to focus on myself. Though the other patients were supportive, I didn't try to make friends.

Friends and family visited me here, and most of the time, I would accept visits and gifts.

My time in the therapy center left me far lighter than I had once been. I was taken apart and put back together halfway. I was released with daily medications to take and a diagnosis of depression and bipolar.

At this point, my TBI was being assessed. The revolving jury of doctors were hung, unable to agree on an assessment. Later on, I had two neurologists in the same city disagree on my diagnosis. One tested and diagnosed me with a TBI where I was awarded social security, and years later, the other said I never had a traumatic brain injury. The basis of their argument was that I was too successful to have suffered a TBI. I had a college degree, I was in a stable relationship (married), and he told me to leave his office and that I no longer in need of his services.

Chapter 5

I walked outside with my family, and I remember what the sun and sky were like. I felt free but imprisoned at the same time, with this head injury, unsure how to handle myself in the real world. My parents told me I would be leaving with them soon on a vacation to see my sister participate in the Miss Teen America Pageant in Nashville, Tennessee. I said I was not interested, but they insisted I went. The family and I prepared, and I packed my clothes but most importantly my own music for me to listen to on the long road trip. I had a bit of a bad attitude but overall improved and trusted and loved a little more each day.

We left our neighborhood in Redmond, Oregon, and trekked across the country to Nashville. We stopped along the way to Precious Moments Farm in Missouri which was awesome and a hot day. We stopped at a really cool Walmart in the Midwest and got clothes. We arrived at the hotel in Nashville. We had the opportunity to check out several horse farms and look at potential stallions for our horse at home in Redmond. The parking lot was filled with motorcycles from a convention at the same time as the pageant. My sister was in tip-top shape. She had all her dresses and shoes and makeup and letterheads with her signature. She did her thing and I did mine. The hotel in the lobby had a river run through it. I begged my dad to take me on the river in a tourist boat. There were shops, restaurants, and shows. Everything was expensive. I spent time with my dad around the shops and walked around. He was patient with my behavior. I had a short and impulsive attention span. I would get nervous with the crowds and walk in patterns. I was just not my normal self. My dad took me to a Nashville country music show and drove around the freeway which was much more modern than I expected. My mom was spending as much time to help my sister as possible. My parents and I toured Tennessee Walker farms and met their famous stallions. The pageant was exciting and controversial. I was so proud of my sister and when she sang her opera in her dress it was such a beautiful experience.

This was not an appropriate setting to treat a head injury. What I needed was immediate head injury treatment, a series of tests, and observations. I underwent an MRI and results showed no major change to my brain tissue. But this didn't mean the damage wasn't there. The head injury was showing itself through my behavior. This where the next step of therapy should be tested by a neurologist, a test of brain capability. Down the road, I was tested for three hours of crazy questions.

"Here are seven words. Remember them and say them back to me and then spell the word and say them backwards. Look at shapes on a piece of paper and then recall them to me. Please ask me if you hear voices."

I said, "Yes, of course. Doesn't everyone hear God's voice?"

As soon as that answer left my mouth I would be questioned for years by doctors. My charismatic Christian upbringing was so strong, normalcy was to hear God in a very natural and sweet way. Of course, I hear God through the Bible, through prayers, and other people's encouragement. At nineteen, though, I was naive to the world of medical psychiatry. I didn't even know what schizophrenia or bipolar disorder was. I figured that God was a part of my life. I had no idea that those words I said would be taken out of context as they were. I didn't speak the cold professional language of these people; I didn't know what was okay to say in front of medical professionals. Thankfully, I was approved after this test and officially declared disabled with a traumatic brain injury. I was awarded with social security in 2010, four long years after my accident and first hospital visit.

Not all the news was good. The doctor of psychiatry at that first hospital wanted to double label me not just with a head injury but bipolar as well. To this day, I do not accept the diagnosis. He sugarcoated it: "Do you know that many movie stars have bipolar disorder and are still successful?"

This conversation left me frustrated. I was so normal before my head injury. I never saw a psychiatrist or knew of any of these diagnoses. I was happy, academic, fit, loving, and in control. I had a stable mood and even reached out to others when they needed calming or cheering up. After the head injury, I withdrew to sadness and confusion that I hadn't known before. Although the side effects from a head injury can be similar to those found in mental illness, they are separate things that should be treated separately and not together. This is exactly how the laws in California work. When I was engrossed into this new world, I was the only one who knew myself, I was the only one who would stick up for me.

For me to sustain a normal existence, I have had to take medications for my brain that they insisted would connect my frontal lobe. They told me I would be rational and organized instead of impulsive. I will practice discretion in this book. I will not refer to any direct medication, name of doctor, or facility. There were three times throughout my life that I took myself off medications for losing weight purposes. In all these cases, I went downhill fast and did not recover until therapy and restabilization back on medications. It was a tough lesson to learn, but I only wanted the things that once came so easily to me.

My regular doctor who knew me before and after the accident sustained a professional opinion that all I had was a head injury. My psychiatric term, however, was a strong strike against me. Being stuck in the mental ward for a few days did not help medical records to support my strictly physical ailment. I will die in my high heels that I had a brain injury in 2006 and that is what changed my behavior and personality nothing else.

# Chapter 6

Summer 2006 was survival mode. I became close with the safe things in my life—books, especially. My mom was reading Christian author novels and I would read one a week. I would dive into the love stories—the lives and adventures of other people. I enjoyed taking my dog on walks. I would run and exercise. I switched churches to a local Baptist church in Redmond. Everything else was kept at a safe distance, not because I was worried about getting hurt, but my mental and emotional capacity was limited. I got nervous in crowds. A super Walmart was built near my house, and I had a hard time going in there because of the things and people I had to look at. Luckily, there was a break from school to get better until fall. I spent a lot of time at home that summer. Friendships were limited to once a month appointment when I would get enough energy and confidence.

During the fall of 2006 I enrolled back into school. I came back overweight after being on medication for the first time, but my mind was alert and ready to learn. However, my social skills, like my appearance, had faded with my injury. I got nervous around everyone, so I hid from conversations and remained focused at school. Being back at school was not like it was before. I was the all-star student when I had first enrolled but was now internally struggling as a student, longing to be happy and normal again. Though I started to trend toward the antisocial, the small Christian novels my mother and I read became an outlet for me. It would help with the escape into a happy world when reality wasn't as happy for me. Some friends stayed with me and they became my crew. We would hang out once a month and on special occasions. They were as supportive as they could. I shared some things with them, but not many.

One unexpected positive note came after the brain injury though. My grades improved from mostly As and a few Bs too straight As until I received my associate degree in the summer of 2007. My brain was quicker with science and math than it was before. I excelled in statistics, computers, and physics. I tested well and tended to grasp concepts fast. No longer was I the student government guru and popular girl on campus but someone else entirely.

The college graduation I had dreamed about for so long came to pass. My hair was curly and blonde like it had usually been. I wore it long with a green dress though I was a bit overweight. My family supported my graduation. I appreciated that. School's journey had seen me go through the scope of my injury. I was able to finish with honors despite my condition. After college, I decided to take a couple years off from school and pursue personal goals and my health. This turned out to be a really good decision. This time was where I really worked on the basics of life to sharpen my mental, physical, and emotional skills.

I decided that I was not going to stay inside and do nothing but use this time wisely. So, I wrote out goals for myself: learn how to surf, take horse riding lessons, play tennis, and keep my mind active. I continued reading and even tried to socialize a bit more. I met with the same group of girls for Bible study around this time. I switched churches back to the one I used to go to. With all these plans, I started to save my money and pay for sport lessons, read and walk my dog. I supported my sister as she was now a senior in high school going to all her concerts, games, and school functions. Over this period of time, my brain comprehension grew tremendously.

I was hired that summer of 2007 as a marketing intern in downtown Bend. At my summer internship, I gained knowledge and experience in the small business community, learning the marketing tools that I applied personally. I had a computer, company phone, and a desk. I worked in the same office as my boss and another guy in the website design business in Bend. I worked with various local businesses: coffee shops, furniture stores, and a catering chef company.

I wrote news releases, an article in a local business newspaper, created marketing ideas, met with clients, and did clerical work.

During this time frame, I was working on my figure. I was losing weight while being on my medications for my brain injury. I have been watching my diet and running a river trail a few times a week since it was summer. Another highlight of this internship was lunch in downtown Bend during the summer. I enjoyed the thirty minutes at noon with a bag lunch by the river. I struggled in deciding if I would mention my head injury to my boss; I decided not to. In order to not feel overwhelmed mentally, I would write to-do lists every morning in order of priority. My boss, during my time there, praised my work and appreciated the help in his business. At the time he needed an intern because business was booming.

At the end of summer, I had saved some money and a group of friends and I went to Redding, California, for a few days to go to the water park. I enjoyed the experience and felt comfortable around these friends when it came to my head injury hang ups. I remained calm and had fun sharing memories. When I returned, I made the choice to continue to work on my personal goals in sports and mental sharpening through books.

I continued to be healthy and meet with health care professionals. My doctor was a big help in monitoring my medicine and thorough explaining what a frontal lobe head injury was and its side effects. She made it clear that life would not be easy, and I would never be the same as before. She said the frontal lobe is the part of your brain that affects behavior, concentration, writing, and personality. In order for my brain to function as normally as possible, I needed medications to close the gap between the part of the brain that connects to the frontal lobe. The medications serve to reconnect the parts of my frontal lobe that were damaged. This prevents depression, anxiety, and other effects of a head injury in the frontal lobe that are displayed through behavior. She explained to me that because I was in school, I should be on medications to stabilize me. She said over the years she wanted to try different medications and see what works and what doesn't and see down the road how I do with each. She said her goal as my doctor was to see me at thirty-five happy, graduated from college, married, and in a job that is perfect for me.

I took up scrapbooking as a hobby and documented everything I did. In the spring of 2008, I took tennis lessons and horse lessons. When summer came, I learned how to surf. I took family trips and was preparing for fall to go to college to complete my bachelor's degree. I got accepted in college and a sorority with my sister. I was thrilled and figured that since I had taken all that time off to be intellectually, emotionally, and socially ready to live on my own. Sadly, I did not know how wrong I was. After my family left me at the sorority emotionally, I broke down quickly. I couldn't concentrate, I even got headaches sometimes, and everything overwhelmed me. Living on my own, even basic needs were a challenge. Eating enough or being able to sleep was not easy. My roommates were great, but they all handled themselves as professional students. Knowing how to time everything: sleep, food, studying, social, and spiritual life. I couldn't do anything right. Even classes were intimidating and the professors' expectations were high. Peers were snooty and didn't give me the time of day. My sorority had planned all these activities and parties. You would think because my sister was there I would be fine? No, everything wasn't fine. I felt on top of everything. I had to watch out for her and be the big sister. She stayed for two years at school and the sorority, but I left and withdrew from college after three weeks. It was so horrible but not too embarrassing because at that point I wanted to be happy and healthy.

When I returned home, I met with my doctors to change and check up with my medications. I was so thankful for my parents. I enrolled back into college in the winter of 2008. I had to go back and do a couple terms at the community college in business so I could get accepted into business school. I completed those courses swiftly. My first class in upper division courses was a soil management course. The concepts were hard for me, but in the end, I got a B+ on my final paper. I switched over to upper division college courses in the middle of the school year and took my first three business classes. It was a long term, but I ended up learning well in the smaller class environment and interacted well with other students. I was getting As and Bs. One thing I am so proud of myself for is that I always kept going in college until I finished. I never stopped because things got too hard even though they did. I persevered.

Chapter 7

In the summer of 2009, my aunt said she wanted to congratulate me early from graduating from college and to save money for a trip. She would take me to Hawaii on December 2009. This was perfect. I finished the winter term well. Another life change I had been praying about for years was working in church ministry. I met with the youth pastors and became a youth leader in the summer of 2009. I was a natural at loving and helping preteen girls. I called them every week for over a year. I headed up a small group every week and tried to stay involved and helped these girls through life. I was even a camp counselor the next summer at the Oregon Coast. For a year and a half, I went to school, Bible study with my friends, youth group, and spent time with my mom and dad every week. I was a girl of habit and had a bit of a comfort zone.

Hawaii was the best vacation opportunity I have ever had. My aunt and I were already very close. She met me at the airport in Maui, and for almost a month, I spent my whole winter vacation with her in Hawaii. She brought me to Lahaina and got a room for three days in a white hotel right on the beach. I thought I walked over to heaven when I entered the room and saw the view. There were two adjacent beds in the normal hotel room. We went right to the beach and took so many wonderful pictures.

The next morning, I went to the surf shop alone because she was a librarian at a middle school and had to work a couple days before her break. I paid for lessons. I got into the water and initially thought it would be warmer, but after five minutes it felt like bath water. I got out to the surf and was told to paddle harder. With a push from my instructor on the back of my board once the wave was right, I stood up the first few times. I was a natural and loved the culture of surfing in general. I did this for two more days and ran out of spending money to do anymore surfing. My aunt took me to a lobster dinner and a luau on the beach in Lahaina. We went to the shops. We love to shop and eat. We met a friend of hers who is an artist and showed us around, sharing a glimpse of her life on the island. Another dear friend of my aunt offered to let us stay at her house for a few days on the golf course. I respect and cherish this woman as a friend now. She carried herself in such a lovely and spunky manner and enjoyed getting to know me. We went with her and her other friends to a dinner luau with Hawaiian dancers and music. I lost weight and was looking healthy and fit. We traveled around the whole island. We explored the hills where we stayed with friends on a farm near the north shore but in the hills. The surfers that hit those waves are crazy. We spent Christmas with this couple. I made Christmas cookies all day for everyone, getting in the Christmas spirit. On the end of the trip, we saw the remote part of the island in Kona where more locals live in. We stayed at a resort and enjoyed the views and drive. We hiked up and saw the sunset at the famous place in Maui early one morning. We went to the Maui Prince a couple of nights. I hurt my foot surfing on some coral and still have a scar there to prove it. A day before my flight home, my dad called saying he was supposed to have given a lecture in my class in business about his job as a quality engineer since we were learning about quality. I realized that I had better hurry home because school had started and I wasn't there.

Two school days later, I had to meet with all my teachers and explained my absence. Everyone understood except for my new marketing teacher. He was a little tough, but his class was like any other. I worked hard and did pretty well. I learned in that class about marketing and writing a marketing plan for a business which was interesting. In college life, I had an attitude that I could do anything, and that attitude carried me through. Spring term went fast and already it was summer of 2010. After the trip and some medicine changes, I had decided that since I was doing pretty well overall to get off the medicine without anyone knowing so I could lose weight.

I was getting older and realized my twenties were flying by, and I didn't feel fit enough. I lost fifty pounds over three months at the cost of everything else. I started to have behavior problems at home, and I would get mad or withdrawn. Sometimes, I would lash out at my parents, and they would try to deal with it in their own way. Their way was to pray for me and make sure I stayed stable on medication. I had trouble concentrating that spring term in school, and sometimes, I would say things that were out of place or even inappropriate. That term, I withdrew from my school. Summer was here and I decided to end my time with the kids. I wanted to end on a good note; I didn't want the children to see how fast my health was deteriorating.

My brother's girlfriend graduated from college in 2007 with a bachelor's degree in horticulture. She and my brother were seriously dating throughout college. A year later, my brother graduated with his bachelor's in economics, business, and accounting—triple major with honors. A year later, he and Angela got married at an historic church in downtown Portland. It was resplendent—family, friends, decorations, flowers, the dress, and the bride. I said some Bible verses at the wedding. We all partied afterward. They bought a house in Lake Oswego a couple years later and have taken trips around the world.

The fall of 2010 was like the season itself—a time of change. I turned twenty-four that year. I changed my hair color from blonde to dark brown/red. I applied for social security and was awarded full benefits: medical and everything. For the first time, I had a steady income. I had just came off my medication and was starting to balance out. But I wasn't healed. I started shopping impulsively. This went on for years until it was cured. I had gotten myself back into pageant shape. I was buying expensive makeup, purses, and clothes. I loved clothes, I loved doing my hair, and I loved the process of it. For purposes of confidentiality, I will not give details of my impulse buying and impulsive behavior. During this time, I received more attention for my outward appearance than ever before, though things were so tumultuous inside my head. I went back to school in the winter of 2010.

I had to withdraw again in the spring of 2010. There was a class that I didn't do well in, and it was all hard for me. I was running one cold spring day to get coffee up a shortcut over a hill with boulders, a shorter alternative than the walkway I would usually take. I fell and broke my left arm's humerus bone. It completely felt like it broke in half by the elbow, like breaking a saltine in half. I felt it dangling by the skin. It hurt like hell, but I stayed brave and students came out to help me. When paramedics arrived, they stabilized my arm. They made a decision to get me to the hospital. They took me by car instead of ambulance for money purposes. The break was bad, and this was a risky decision. All I remember was the next morning waking up to my mom being there by my side and drinking an amazing strawberry banana smoothie. The surgery had already taken place and was the second hardest surgery out of one thousand the doctor had performed. This is because the elbow has a nerve which could have been fatal if the break was any closer to it.

Chapter 8

I went back to school over another couple years. One class at a time. Whether online or at the academy, I kept going. Finally, I finished my bachelor's degree in business administration. I graduated in the summer of 2012 in Corvallis, and First Lady Michelle Obama gave the commencement speech. By my time of graduation, I had let myself get out of shape again.

Around this time, my friends were changing. My friends who had been so dear to me decided to go different ways. I have not been able to retain most of those relationships throughout the years. After the arm break, I met a lady who tried to help me. She was nice, and there was so much change with my arm, limiting my capabilities physically that I clung to her for awhile. But as time would show, she had her own problems which led us to part ways. I transitioned out of the church where I had served and been happy for a total eight years. I moved onto a little Baptist church in Bend for the summer and then settled on another Christian church in Bend that is grounded but has a younger influence. The pastor still keeps me on my toes with his messages. People are friendly there but left enough distance for me to interact with them slowly.

My parents urged me to find love after I finished my degree. As providence would have it, I met my husband that year. We met at a bar downtown during the summer of 2012, right after the movie theatre shooting in Colorado. We talked back and forth, and he asked me to go to the movie late at midnight. I said I was scared after the shooting, but he said he would protect me. I thought he was comely and a hard worker so I said yes to the date. I got into his car and went to the movies. We had instant chemistry in the movies, and it was the best movie experience I ever had. The movie seemed so realistic and my company was so exciting. I invited him over for pizza and a living room showing of James Cameron's *Titanic* later that week. We went with my dog the following week for a hike. The next few days, I went to Las Vegas with my aunt and cousin to celebrate my graduation.

My driving was dangerous for a while. Sometimes, medications would affect my driving and I would struggle with road rage. I would pass cars close and speed around them all while getting angry. On the way to get ready the day of my trip to Las Vegas, a police officer stopped by my house and said that he had over one hundred complaints of my driving. I talked with him respectfully, and he said as long as I didn't get any more complaints, I would be okay. An hour or so later, I was on my way to the airport to meet my aunt and cousin in Las Vegas.

On the trip, my mind was consumed and excited for the new man in my life. I thought about how cute he was and how instantaneous our friendship and connection had been. He told me to bring him back something from the trip. When I arrived at the airport, my aunt, cousin, and I took a picture with a professional photographer with props and a fun backdrop. We went to our hotel in New York, New York. On my bed was a letter and laminated card that said "celebrate." We set out all our clothes as girls do and chatted a bit. Then, we went down to the poolside and laid out in the sun and got in the water. The hotel was fancy with livery all around. I enjoyed talking with my cousin. She is one of the smartest people I know. I have always looked up to her.

Later that evening, we got dressed in our evening attire and went out to town. There was a good Elvis impersonator. We went to a dance club called Coyote where the girls danced on tables in bar attire, getting the crowd to dance and have fun. Later on, I got asked to dance on the table with some of the girls in my high heels. Everyone laughed, and it was an interesting experience for me as an adult spending time with my family. We went around Las Vegas the following day, checking out the town. The shopping was cool. I bought a dress and earrings and took a picture in front of a fancy purse shop. We had dinner at an opera in an open square. We saw a concert outside, but all the performers did short performances. I found a dollar with John Cena on it for the new man in my life, and one with Michael Jackson for me. On the plane ride home, I had a beer at a bar in the airport, and when I went back to get on my flight everyone was gone in the waiting area and the loudspeaker announced, "Last chance Elsibeth Hoyt for flight to Portland, Oregon." So, I ran to the plane, and we took off back home.

I was excited to see this new man again. I think he was a little disappointed I didn't get him a sweatshirt. I think I could see in his eyes, but he got it that we had just met and I had gotten him something to show that I was thinking of him on my trip. We spent the next month with each other all the time. We would grab some beer and hang out at his place while he played video games and then watch a movie. We would go to the park or JC's where we meet and walk around downtown, getting to know each other. I was living with my parents, so we spent most of our time getting to know each other in Bend. We would go hiking in Bend through different trails and go to the Butte which offered pristine views of town. We did some shopping at Macy's, I showed him clothes that looked good on him, and bought him a few staple items. Over the course of us dating and developing a friendship, he asked me to be his girlfriend in early September. I enjoyed dressing up for him and always tried to apply makeup. It was nice to have someone to dress up for again.

Chapter 9

We decided to take a three-day trip to the Oregon Coast. We took my dog, which he loved, and we saved our money to leave in September 2012. These were the salad days, puppy love. We couldn't stop talking, laughing, and kissing. On the way there, once we reached the coast, we took a picture that became our hallmark as a couple. We stopped to eat at this bear-themed diner on the way to the Coast in remote Oregon. We read facts about Oregon while we ate. We stopped another time at a restaurant with carousels and mermaids decorating the interior. I remember the food was phenomenal. Along the coastal highway, we stopped at beaches and shops. We went to the Aquarium in Newport, and Mario was taking pictures like crazy of all the ocean life. We paid to get a professional picture done there. There was a shop that had used dresses and Mario bought me one. We signed our names and the date on the wall outside the dress shop like a couple of teenagers. Our first night camping was at a lake an hour from Florence. Our second night was along the coast off the ocean, and our final night at Seal Rocks Campground which had an incredible view. I learned more about him and him me. We walked and talked along the beach and shared many memories.

Throughout the summer and even a year earlier, I had applied to live in many apartments in Bend, Oregon. I had not gotten accepted because they were all low-income that I qualified for on my social security, and there were waitlists. In October, I planned to move and signed a contract for an apartment that would take all my money for rent with a little leftover for living expenses. One week before I was ready to move in, I got a call from some apartments that I was next on the waitlist and could move within a week. Rent was $200 which would leave me $400 for living expenses every month, so I took it and moved in the week of Halloween. My man and I loved Halloween. I was Marilyn Monroe and he was Al Capone.

I moved into my new place and got settled. When my man was at work or doing his thing, I would make my place a home. I got used to living on my own, keeping myself busy with cooking, decorating, and reading. I had a VCR in the beginning, so I watched a bunch of movies. It always made me feel safe. I liked organizing my clothes and shoes and looking through my scrapbooks. Then, Mario and I would split time hanging out between his and my place.

With my head injury, being in a relationship was overall good. It taught me to consider others, which made me happy and thankful. When I got stressed or in a disagreement, I would get angrier than normal. I think it was a combination of my injury and the powerful emotions that come with developing a serious relationship. The following year proved to be very difficult for my health and set me back on my progress. In early spring, my boyfriend and I decided that I should go off my medicine for a while. Things were going so well that I no longer saw the need for it. This is something I never recommend doing. It is very dangerous for head injury patients. I did not know my own limitations.

For my birthday week in April, I drove to Corvallis to visit my sister for a few days. We had good sister bonding time. We went around campus and to church. I had been off the medicine for six weeks, but because I was in a stressful setting and alone, I started to decline in my mental and emotional health. I was stressed, confused, and got angry quickly, making decisions in the spur of the moment without a second thought. I drove home in my 1993 Nissan Sentra that was not always reliable. It was pouring rain and my windshield wipers stopped working.

I pulled off the road and waited it out. I found a mechanic shop to stop at, but it was late, and the shop was closed. Somehow, I got back to my sister's place and took it to a mechanic the following day.

That day, after a well-deserved Starbucks, I hit trouble on the road again. I had no traction tires or chains, and I hit ice over the pass. I pulled over and realized my phone was with my sister and I had to go to the bathroom so bad that I had the worst accident ever. A truck full of guys pulled over, and one of them mentioned that I had an accident. I was a bit scared of them looking rough and said that I was fine and did not need help, so they went on their way. I made a sign with no phone available in my car window on the side of the road needing help. Finally, a nicely dressed lady said she thought I could make it down a snowy patch if she followed behind me slowly. I went along with the idea and got through it and made it home.

I went to Macy's and bought clothes and got ready to meet my boyfriend at a nice restaurant for my birthday. It was my birthday, so I was trying to have a blast and not show how upset I was. Over the course of a few days I was not myself, I lost weight because I was off the medicine for a while and all the recent stress I had gone through. I started having physical pain because my body was adjusting to rapid weight loss.

After I got mad one day and left my boyfriend's house in a huff, I walked toward home which was not far from his house. I stopped at McDonalds and was not feeling well. I started feeling dizzy and couldn't walk so I asked for an ambulance. This sounds drastic now, but at the time it strangely made sense. I was admitted and taken to the emergency room. I was in pain. I remember not being able to feel part of my body, and after a while, I could not explain what was going on with me. I just knew I needed to reach out for help immediately.

I remember going to the same place I had been in the hospital I had worked so hard to leave before: the mental ward. When I arrived, I was physically in pain and aware that whatever was going on I was alone again. It took days and I was not as calm this time. I was reading my legal rights in my room and kept care of myself and ate. I continued to lose weight until I could fit in all the small "hospital prison scrubs." I was eventually placed in the care of the therapy center again. Some of the same staff were there and some were new. I got settled and felt better quickly. I went to treatment classes, ate good meals, and had a regular visitor. You have to take care of yourself and know yourself before you start talking about other people in your life. However, my boyfriend came with roses every few days, and at the end of the time, he met with the medical professionals.

Eventually, in May 2013, my boyfriend came not only to give me a rose but to take me away from the therapy center in his car and into the free world. He and I did well for a bit around each other, but I will never know what made him stay with me and help me through this time. I think it was hard for him to see me like this. Summer got even harder. I was having physical health problems. I read all the time, watched movies, ate little, and tried to sleep.

Over time, I was not feeling well physically. I started shutting down. My boyfriend still came around occasionally which gave me some peace, but I stopped eating regularly, sleeping, and phased in and out of taking my medications. I was unhealthy mentally. Later, I talked with doctors about this time in my life. I was not regular with my medication or sleeping or eating for almost two months, and my mind was affected. I would think things that were not true. My idea of reality was distorted. I closed myself off from the outside world and kept no contact with friends or family during this time. I lived in a world that was not real. In early September, I was found by paramedics in a room in my apartment partially clothed with a day-old bowl of Lucky Charms cereal. They brought me to the hospital in an ambulance. This was the fulcrum on which my life began to move upward. I was back in the mental ward, but my physical and mental state improved after I went back on medications and to some therapy. I eventually got well enough to go back to the therapy center at the hospital. This place was socially hard to get used to again, but I did over a few days by staying quiet and keeping to myself.

People are in that facility for an array of reasons, some more serious than others. But most realize that everyone is getting help. In the mental ward, I was assigned an attorney to help argue my case in court and prove myself. It was unfair to bring a person like this to me until my health was better. She came in off and on in the therapy center as well. Distortions of reality was the hardest thing to overcome on my path to getting better. When you're sick physically and mentally, your mind is the only getaway that makes you feel better. So stories or ideas I would think up became what I thought was true. Overtime, with therapy and correct medications, I was able to sort through these distortions.

Therapy at the "center" was not as helpful the third time around. I had only been in here a few months prior. So, I skipped some therapy sessions but took my medication, ate, and slept great. I remember there was a day that a visitor wanted to see me. A person that had caused me confusion and hurt my feelings, my boyfriend. I agreed to see him. When he came in having spent a lot of his hard-earned money on roses, appearing humble and sorry, I forgave him instantaneously. We had talked the few months prior about getting engaged. We had gotten rings, and he and I decided we wanted to spend the rest of our lives together in the spring when I was at the therapy center. My hard-hit health hadn't changed our love for each other. During some visits I would refuse to see him because I was tired or didn't have extra energy to take care of anyone but myself. This was hard on him. When I did see him, I shortened visits to ten minutes because of my attention span. But most visits were nice, and the staff normally had a "no physical contact" rule with visitors, and they knew we were engaged so we were given our privacy. I met with doctors. I was permitted to leave if I would get regular care at a new health facility that would monitor me more often through the county.

Chapter 10

When I left the therapy center, I had gotten in touch with my family and friends and started to plan my wedding. I spent three months saving, working with the florist, renting a facility, getting a dress, and all the other things involved with planning a wedding. On December 12, 2013, he and I were married. His parents could not be there because they lived in Mexico. My parents, some family on both sides, and select friends filled a room of thirty guests to celebrate the joining of two people that would walk through life together. He surprised me with my ring of choice at the ceremony. I loved dancing with him and taking pictures with all the guests.

Marriage is fun and hard work. I had much more stuff than he did, and he wanted me to declutter before we moved in together. Decorating the house could be stressful trying to find a place for everything and not break things was hard. He wanted me to change up cooking from potatoes, veggies, and meat to homemade tortillas. So down the road I learned, and the hardest thing for me has been cooking, but recently I did a varied meal plan with homemade tortillas every week. Feeling sexy in marriage is important, and although I do because I am a beautiful person on the inside, the outside still needs a little work. Sometimes, due to my medications and working so much, my sex drive can be a bit low. I have learned to control my anger more and detach a bit in arguments in the heat of the moment and to be rational in expressing my emotions and feelings later on. It is hard to understand a person and be understood. He and I try to do something nice for each other and go out. Our favorite restaurants reconnect our bond. We like to go to movies and walk in the park.

In most of our downtime from working, he plays video games and I relax.

Recently, my overall health has been better. Medications have helped my mood and brain function to the point where I can function with a degree of normalcy. Rarely do I struggle with my thoughts except for the occasional discouraging thought or anger. I never want to hurt myself or others. I have a hard time controlling my anger now. It's difficult to realize that it's just an emotion and not overreacting. Cooking, as I mentioned, can be hard because I am not very good or natural at it, so I must work extra hard. I can keep up with cleaning and being domestic, but I must make time. Exercise and nutrition have been important to me lately. As emotional and mental health go, I must love myself and stay true to myself no matter what is going on around me.

When I left the hospital, my husband and I went directly to this care facility called the Annex. I would see my doctor, nurse practitioner, therapist, job specialist, nurse, and nutritionist at the Annex. Each of these people have helped me so much and continue to help me every week to this day. My doctor is smart and caring, running physical tests when I need them. My nurse practitioner is specialized in psychiatric medications. She really understood and helped me explain myself to myself right after the hospital and has been working with me closely for two years with my meds. My therapist and I had an instantaneous connection. I tell her everything and she walks through life with me. My job specialist is a smart man who does his job with the intention of helping anyone get work. I did not start looking for work until February 2014, and I got a job within a week as a cashier. Later, I got a second job as a caregiver and worked about sixty hours a week. The nurse staff checks with my meds and discusses what I'm doing week to week. Sometime during the fall of 2014, I wanted to lose weight in a healthy way, so I met with a nutritionist and devised a plan. Currently, my health is strong. With all these staff members, my husband and I decided that I am going to be monitored so I can come off of all medicine by fall of 2015 while continuing therapy.

On December 2014, I got into a car accident right near where we live. A car hit my car while I was at a stop waiting to turn into our condo complex. She was going fast, and rear ended me. She totaled my car, but it was drivable, so I drove my car till I saved enough money for a new one. In April 2015, I bought my dream car, a 2000 ML Mercedes. I got physical therapy for my back and neck, but overall did not have any severe injuries from the accident. In the summer of 2014, Mario and I went to the beach twice and to the county fair as well as the rodeo. In the summer of 2015, we went to the Sisters Rodeo and enjoyed his family for two weeks while his mother visited from Mexico. Mario's family are sweet and hardworking people who are funny and who love each other. I couldn't ask for more.

Chapter 11

I was inspired to write a book originally by my mother after my head injury. She thought I could help other people and inspire them. Since the hospital, I had a hard time understanding how my case would help serve the injustice and pave the way for change. This year, I watched Disney's Pixar's *Inside Out* in the theater with a friend and her child. In this movie, the emotions in a child's brain are cartoon characters and run her life. Memories are marble balls organized throughout the brain. Forgotten thoughts go to this valley and never come back. I thought how most my thoughts and memories after the accident were forgotten and how it was hard to feel emotions. When I got home and put music on, I came up with the line "head injuries for Jesus" as a book and a nonprofit.

My next relapse was during my marriage recently. I was overwhelmed with work and my marriage. Miraculously, Mario's mom came from Mexico in the summer which brought us closer together. After lots of family parties and work at the end of October, I had the incident. I took my monthly trip to Phagans to get my hair styled and makeup done. For the first time at Phagans I had a facial. The room had white paint and towels with multiple women. I was exposed when I got my robe on. I was embarrassed while having all these personal pressures placed on me and it was too much, so I asked for the service to stop. I paid out and got picked up by my therapist. My therapist picked me up and called my husband then took me back to his office where I waited for my husband. Mario picked me up after work and brought me home.

I knew at this point it might take three months to overcome this incident. This proved to be true. My parents were called, and they came a few days later and took me for a week's vacation to Lyle, Washington, a small town in the gorge. My dad took me to an ice hockey game which our team won. It was a true bonding experience. It showed me that my parents cared although they did not understand everything. I just needed a breather. Still, there would be harder times ahead.

The hardest day of my life started with a stubbed toe. It broke and so did I. On a nice fall day, Halloween 2015, I attempted suicide. I spent what was left in my bank account to feel freedom while my husband at work unknowingly. I drove toward California in my new dress. I ordered lunch to go with sparkling water. I headed one hundred miles outside Bend and ended up at an Indian reservation. I found a hotel in a small town. I turned on the TV, and in total fear and desperation called 911 through the hotel and then my parents. Later, I would find my husband called 911 after I missed work and filed a missing person's report in Klamath County on my behalf. I don't know what was in my head so far from home in that small-town hotel, but I knew if I survived till morning I would live. I did. I got in my car, had some coffee, got gas, and went home to Bend as if the previous day had all been a bad dream.

I drove to a friend's house near our condo. He and a police officer found us. He took me home. He was mad. "I would never do that to you. I was so worried. I love you." I said, "I know you would not, and I am not asking you to forgive me." Later that day after he left for work, I called 911 impulsively and got a ride to the hospital about my toe and reached out to get some help.

The police gave me a ride after the 911 call ride and dropped me off at the ER voluntarily. I reported the head injury to the ER (which never gets taken seriously) and my broken toe. I was torn when I saw my husband in the ER. My tough facade fell, and I fell into his arms in tears. His love for me and my respect for him in this health scare left me in awe. The doctors did not know what to do with me, with all things being similar to the other experiences they had with me after a few hours in the ER they placed me in the mental ward.

I said goodbye to Mario the first time in the lockdown psychiatric ward. Though I was married, I feared that I would be alone and forgotten. Despite this, I showed no fear for the week I was there until the therapy center opened. The therapy center was fun. I had an allergy to the medicine and had to go back to the mental ward for three days. During this time, one man escaped his cell and was raging about the food and managed to trigger my posttraumatic stress disorder. I watched a movie in a side room and played a portable video game which helped calm me down. I would always shower, brush my hair, take care of my teeth, and be nice to other people. I was able to receive the guide in Central Oregon for winter activities and dreamed briefly about being let out to enjoy the world.

Once I was at the therapy center, I read books and took care of my hair, which were my main goals. Therapy groups were helpful. The dance and outdoor therapy classes were my favorite. There are three meals a day and quite a bit of freedom. You don't have to go to groups, but they are helpful. I took my journal and wrote everything. Between my journal and classes, I learned various things. I journaled my résumé so when I got out of therapy I could maintain a job.

My sister was super sweet and visited me with her boyfriend, a premed student who works at the hospital. They brought me gifts—a blanket and clothes and a jimbay drum so I could sing. My parents visited me a couple times. I was worried as a business graduate that they could not sell their rental in this difficult housing market. They had a ranch that they were eyeing, and I was excited about the prospect. I talked to other patients about getting it going. One of the patients was my friend. We would go to groups and eat meals together and take in the fitness classes. I was what you might refer to as an alpha female in the hospital. I always wanted my way, I wanted to be happy although I was alone. Being alone gave me time to reflect on my life and become stronger this time around. I did not feel hopeless but felt rested because of the resources given to me in this tumultuous time.

In the middle of my stay, I drew a picture of me riding on my surfboard on the back of my Mercedes SUV parked in the parking lot of my husband's place. A book on energy type I read on the bookshelf from the hospital was written by a doctor. I found out that I am adaptive and aggressive. When I first enter a new place like a workplace or school, I make a point to get acquainted ASAP. This proved to be true during my stay with my parents in Lyle, Washington.

Positive self-talk statements include the following:

- I am a lovable capable person
- I dare to be myself
- I am learning a sense of balance
- I choose to live fully in the present.

The therapy classes were sometimes interesting and occasionally a chore just like school.

At the start of every morning at 8:00 a.m., we would meet to discuss one goal for the day. For mine, I always chose a shower just because I was being a smartass and didn't want to be there or around those people but with my family who loved me. My parents, brother, sister, husband, mother-in-law, and niece.

I planned in my head what I would do for the day and kept my mind filled with the hip-hop music that we got to listen from the personal radios.

The days were highly regimented. At 9:00 a.m. was DBT skills, like practical skills. Then REC at 11:00 a.m. and 2:00 p.m. I was stuck in the first snows of the winter. I was there voluntarily so I could walk around outside by myself for fun. Then 1:00 p.m. came, and it was time for psychotherapy. It was a time to unwind from your current situation and get a plan together for your eventual release. After that it was 6:00 p.m. recovery and self-care and at 7:00 p.m. was mindfulness. Fridays were movie nights, and among the features that I saw were *Mr. and Mrs. Smith* (kind of risqué) and *Date Night* with Steve Carell.

Here are some highlights of classes I remember. In the appendix, I will put detailed reports from the class's higher learners and from the teachers at the therapy center.

Ride the Wave: ways that I get knocked down and washed over by my emotions are looks, like not looking good enough, or looking too tall and curvy. Not enough money at Christmas time or in my marriage or not having enough money to provide the life I want with my husband. Ways I can keep my balance to "Ride the Wave" of my emotions is surfing and riding the wave of my emotions. These skills will be useful to me because of my Mercedes SUV with the surfboard rack.

If you were going off the map what would you put in a bag? I said flax seeds and a Wii dance CD. Ways I will use this stuff: I will use these things to get a job and restore things with Mario.

20 Ways to Practice Gratitude: Benefits of gratitude are:

- Those who journal gratitude are 25% happier than those who did not according to UCAA Gratitude Research.
- Being less self-centered, giving respect to others.
- According to the Dalai Lama, this is an opener to locked up blessings.
- Be on speaking terms with happiness and your heart.
- Do a random act of kindness.

I am grateful for the following in this moment: sunrise, sunset, butterflies, birds, healing, honey, herbs, bees, flowers, kindred spirits, my mind, my body, my soul, community, relationships, art, music, passion, creativity, Mother Earth, clean air, family, friends, health, sun, sisters, awesome parents, work, rest, play, food, medicine, clean water, teachers, school, and memories.

Radical Acceptance: Only you can control yourself. The successes I have are my music and songwriting, hard fashion, rodeo drive, and having enough.

Spiritual Class was led by a Jewish Rabbi. In the previous session at the therapy center, I told the rabbi that got engaged to Mario, and I was scared with so many questions and prayers. At this time, I asked the same guy about being separated from the man I love. He told me to pick the one I am best at spiritually and worst from this alphabetical list. My best is attention. Pay attention. Stay awake and totally alert.

See with receptive eyes and discover a world of ceaseless wonders. I did this at the therapy center by listening to music, enjoying my shower, and styling my hair. Faith is what I have struggled with since traumatic brain injury for over ten years. Ways to combat this fact is to recognize and accept that there is another dimension to life than what is obvious to us. Live with obstacles, doubt, and paradox, knowing that God is always present in the world.

Relationships/relationship thinking: This skill is designed to help you hold multiple perspectives and viewpoints because while reality can be black and white, most instances in life occur in shades of grey. In relationships, there are partial truths in each person's perspective, especially when the viewpoints are in conflict. This skill is appreciating other opinions by tolerating and acknowledging mistakes. Caring even when you are annoyed or frustrated through being collaborative.

Being effective in relationships (my marriage): Fewer effective strategies that get in the way of having what I want in my relationships are insecurity with weight and my surroundings. More effective strategies are my coping skills: reading, listening to music, and working out. Since being in the hospital for the last two months I have read two books: *Amish Love Story* and *Financial Peace University.* Currently listening to Michael Jackson. Workout: twice a day for a half hour by taking a hike and doing fifty crunches.

Less effective strategies that get in the way of me having a healthy sense of self respect: eating too much. I don't have a regular appetite but sleeping well and eating regular meals helps in my recovery and leads to success in relationships and marriage. Mario's biggest concern is that I am insecure around other girls which I argue I am not. I believe I am curvy and fierce. I am not a great cook (this is true), but I can follow a basic recipe. We love each other, and at the end of day, this is only a three-month separation. We are both working on ourselves trying to be better to ourselves and each other.

On release day, I got on a bus with the belongings I came with and got dropped off downtown. I did not want to be picked up by my husband or my parents, so this worked out. I went to my appointment and went home with my parents in Lyle, Washington, after about six weeks of hospitalization.

Around the holidays, it was hard without my husband. I knew it was the most rational choice for me in the time being. I enjoyed Christmas with my family and attended a high-end engineer Christmas party for my father. There was an open bar, but because I respect my parents' values, I did not drink. I interacted with some of the engineers and met the owners.

In our home environment I helped wash dishes, did some light cooking, and did some cleaning for my parents. I am healing now, so there are few words to describe how I feel other than steady, calm, and thankful to be living. I am thankful that my life was not taken from me on Halloween of 2015.

After staying with my parents, I transitioned to living with my husband in January 2016. It started off well and has continued to be better for me. He and I have both matured and worked on things. Coming together is much more functional and stable than it has been in the past. We do movie nights, date nights, and walks. My husband compliments me daily and I support him fully. I go to bimonthly meetings at a head injury group called Abilitree. The coordinator cooks fabulous meals, and a group of about twenty-five traumatic brain injury survivors discuss our lives before and after the head injury and our ways of coping. I am feeling stable, and I see my attending doctor and go to my therapy appointments every month. Keeping the lines of communication with friends and family and medical professionals keep me healthy.

Work is a stabilizer for me. Although I am not able to work 60-80 hour a week like I did last year, work still plays an important role in my life. In the last few months, I have been working both of my jobs as a cashier and caregiver about 45 hours a week. I love all the people I meet through both of my jobs. The merchandise I sell is intricate and always gives me tons of creative ideas and inspiration. On the caregiving side of things, I have a fabulous client who I am a companion for. I help with cooking, cleaning, and taking them to doctor appointments. I support them with my experiences that I have been through medically. Whether it is work or school, I would encourage anyone who has experienced a head injury to continue in their pursuits. Sometimes, lifestyle modifications are necessary in order to achieve these goals, but the benefits far outweigh the costs.

My intent in sharing my story is to encourage, not to discourage anyone with head injuries. My point is to share my story with honesty and integrity. Life is not always easy; it can be hard but that's okay. I think it takes courage to reflect on one's journey through recovery. The story is not as simple as a winning glory. Sometimes, you don't win the day, the hour, or the minute. The courage comes from getting up and trying your best every day. I tackle new goals that are reasonable. I am motivated to help myself and others. I never give up. I feel blessed I am able to work, be married, and be happy most of the time. I am fortunate to be writing this story for the world. You should know that you can overcome any obstacle. Be honest with yourself and others. Keep fighting the good fight. Be the best you can.

Chapter 12

With the heart to research all of these traumatic brain injury topics and correlate them with my story, I hope that it may inspire and help others. I am still the same person; I just live with the effects of a traumatic brain injury. The most recent effect for me has been fatigue. A technique I use to combat this is to get moving and not let it get to me. Other times, I need to rest and take time for myself. To understand a head injury at all is to grasp the medical and scientific definition of the term.

There has been a journal online through my journey of research for this book called "Traumatic Brain Injury Survival Guide" by Dr. Glen Johnson, Clinical Neuropsychologist. "The Brain and How it Works" is also a good place to start. "Weighing only 3 pounds…100 billion cells…Some parts of the brain will work fine while others are in need of repair or are slowly being reconnected" (Johnson 2010, http://tbiguide.com). The human brain is so complex to fathom. Endeavoring to understand it, however, is what brings me closest to understanding my own. On my MRI there was no damage. But from my behavior change, it was apparent that there was an impact on the frontal lobe of my brain later confirmed by a neurologist. I think my brain was in need of repairs and reconnection. Medication has assisted my journey in functioning normally. From how my doctor explained it, medication helped connect damaged cells in my brain in order for them to function normally. The medicine helps damaged neurons that are supposed to send out chemicals that register to the brain what emotions are being felt. "Each of the billions of neurons 'spit out' chemicals that trigger other neurons…like epinephrine, norepinephrine, or dopamine" (Johnson 2010). When I hear information, I remember things, but I have to work on it. In researching how information is received in the brain I have found that "Information enters from the spinal cord and comes up the middle of the brain. It branches out like a tree and goes to the surface of the brain" (Johnson 2010). The frontal lobe part of the brain was where I was impacted which is the surface of the brain behind the forehead. "The biggest and most advanced part of the brain is the frontal lobe" (Johnson 2010). Most advanced is another term for unknown and hard to understand. "Neurosurgery could stop behavioral problems such as violence. The problem was that patients stopped doing a lot of other things. They didn't take care of themselves and they stopped many activities of daily living" (Johnson 2010). The fact that a person would damage the brain on purpose baffles. God gives us a gift of life including our brain and personality. I remember not being able to take care of myself at the worst of my head injury. This is so real and true. "Individuals with frontal lobe impairment seem to lack motivation and have difficulty doing any task that requires multiple steps…there is a breakdown in the ability to sequence and organize" (Johnson). I did so much daily activity in school and work before the injury and that's why everything came to a halt afterward. After time and practice, I could slowly add more to my plate. Emotions play such an important part of life. According to Johnson, "The frontal lobe also plays an important role in controlling emotions. Deep in the middle of the brain are sections that control emotions. They're very primitive emotions that deal with hunger, aggression, and sexual physical drive. These areas send messages to other parts of the brain to do something. If you're mad, hit something and eat it. The frontal lobe "manages" emotions. In general, the frontal lobe has a NO or STOP function. If your emotions tell you to punch your boss, it's the frontal lobe that says STOP or you're going to lose your job. People have often said to me a little thing will set me off and then I'm really mad. The frontal lobe failed to stop or turn off the emotional system." I would say that in the way my mind was impacted, I would rely on my emotions to send me messages like instincts of how I felt about doing something: do I want to sit here, move here, talk with this person, be happy, be mad, be sad? After my recovery, I would rely on my brain to think and respond with an emotion rather than forming a quick instant emotional response like before. In general, frontal lobe damage to my brain made a lot more sense once I knew more how the brain worked.

Chapter 13

In understanding common indicators of a head injury, most cases are more apparent than mine. These are headaches, memory, word finding, fatigue, changes in emotion, changes in sleep, environmental overload, impulsiveness, concentration, distraction, and organization. An indicator can be headaches. I never had any headaches per se. Sometimes, I felt a slight pressure or tingling in the temples of my forehead. Here are some questions regarding common indicators according to Johnson's research from the chapter "Common Indicators of a Head Injury."

"Do you have pain in the temples of the forehead?" For them, it was the other indicators that were more apparent. Another indicator can be memory. "Does your memory seem worse following the accident or injury?" Memory was a strong realistic indicator in my case. My memory got stronger as I practiced and spent extra time at it through studying and reading a variety of books. "Do you have difficulty coming up with the right word?" Due to being in college at the time after my injury I was reading frequently, so word finding was a challenge I overcame fast. I would learn overtime to talk a little less to prevent word finding problems under pressure. I learned to talk in public or professional situations with previously crafted outlines detailing what and how I would present. Fatigue is a problem. "Do you get tired more easily (mentally) and or physically?" Fatigue and being tired is a side effect of medications I have taken. Before the accident, I had much more energy and was rarely fatigued. After the accident, fatigue was a lifestyle change. I was tired all the time. This fatigue affected me socially, and academically in terms of what I could accomplish. Changes in emotion is one of the hardest obstacles I have faced with my injury. "Are you more easily irritated or angered, quickly?" I was very stable and in control of my emotions before my head injury. After I get irritated or angry, it becomes hard to control the anger. The emotion occurs more often within me then it had before my injury. When I lived with my parents, I would get frustrated easily and be more vocal with my emotions. It is also harder to gauge another person's emotions when they are mad at you and to not overreact to them. "Do you cry or become more depressed easily?" Depression hit me hard due to other side effects from the injury like weight gain, lack of motivation, and a decreased social aptitude. Over time, I had to accept and appreciate the new me. I'll never be my old self, but I am stronger and better at overcoming my hardships, and better at learning the coping skills required to function competitively in society. Another common indicator is changes in sleep. "Do you keep waking up throughout the night and early morning and can't get back to sleep?" During one of my episodes after meeting my future husband I struggled with changes in my sleep. Over a period of time, not sleeping severely affected my ability to function with normalcy. Insomnia affected my mental health and my ability to take care of my basic needs such as eating and taking care of myself. Not sleeping regularly becomes an extreme problem over time. In order to not relapse, I take my sleep very seriously now and do not allow myself to not get adequate sleep. Environmental overload is a reality that I and other head injury patients have had to cope with. "Do you find yourself easily overwhelmed in noisy or crowded places?" This struggle was evident soon after the head injury. For about a year or two, the places I felt overwhelmed included large family gatherings, Walmart, and family vacations. The feeling of being overwhelmed was a natural stressor in my brain which could not handle the pressures of appearance, questions, and stressful situations. Impulsiveness is "If you find yourself making poor or impulsive decisions" (Johnson 2010). After the head injury, I struggled with compulsive shopping. I made quick decisions socially. I remained stable in school as I taught myself to be normal and remain calm under pressure. Concentration is one of the frontal lobe functions that can be disrupted by injury. "Do you have difficulty concentrating?" In order to finish two degrees after my head injury, concentration was something I had to discipline myself to do. With discipline and time, I slowly regained my ability to concentrate. I read books in my spare time to help me focus better. After a head injury it is common to be easily distracted. "Are you easily distracted?" Distraction for me was a matter of studying for short periods of time and taking breaks to prevent distraction; I knew my limits. Organization is yet another frontal lobe area affected by my injury. "Do you have difficulty getting organized or completing a task?" I think organization is connected to how much you can accomplish. I used to get so much done in a day before the head injury. But after my injury, I had to understand myself and what I could accomplish. I did organize myself to an extent after the head injury but on a smaller scale. Instead of doing everything, I would prioritize the most important things. Common indicators for traumatic brain injuries are important to personalize a person's specific injury to see that what you are going through is normal and there are ways to overcome these obstacles and still be successful in life.

Chapter 14

Different stages of emotional recovery will occur. Confusion and agitation right after the accident is described as, "be[ing] somewhat dazed for a few minutes" (Johnson 2010). While I was snowboarding down Mt. Hood from the summit gaining speed, I was nearly to the bottom when I hit a small bump and patch of ice going between 25–40 mph. I remember falling into the snow and then I blacked out, regaining consciousness after a few minutes. At that point, I did feel dazed for about three hours. This period included getting up, talking with my uncle and his friend, and driving home to Central Oregon. Slowly, my dazed state transformed into a confused one for about six weeks. "When they wake up, they may go through the confused and agitated state . . . for 99% of patients this stage goes away" (Johnson 2010). This stage for the patient is real and hard to cope with. After the six weeks of confusion, I underwent a year of agitation. I was agitated because I wanted to finish college faster, compete in pageants, and have my figure back. I wanted to have the respect back from my peers and function as I did before in my church. I felt very alone and had to re-evaluate myself at what I gained confidence and self-esteem from.

Chapter 15

Denial can be more common in some cases than others. I faced my situation head on because at that time in my life I was so occupied with school, pageants, work, volunteer work, church, and sports that it was evident after my accident I could not function and have the same result as before the accident. "For some people they don't get better. They wonder why they are doing some silly things. They have these odd events and keep rationalizing them away" (Johnson 2010). I was this person for three years. I would do something a bit out of character but try to surround myself with people or situations where I wouldn't care as much or where I could find more acceptance. When your brain reacts to an emotion, an action immediately occurs right away if you don't relearn to control it. For instance, in church, I assumed a pastor wanted to talk with me at any moment and just burst into the office without warning. Rarely I would want to vocalize myself in class, but I realized that in most cases I should just wait to talk with the teacher one on one. Later in college, I would only ask a question or pipe in a comment pertinent to the topic of discussion. In the first year of my injury, especially, I would be embarrassed of my behavior on occasion, and instead of rationalizing it away, I would just die inside. Family and those helping me at the time would always say, "Well, you're doing this because of the head injury or the medication."

Over time, this annoyed me. I am still a normal person you can confront about issues without attaching my head injury on a case-by-case basis. There are two types of denial that head injury survivors face. "The first type of denial is an emotional one. Something that has happened that is so terrible, so frightening that they just don't want to deal with it" (Johnson 2010). I think a person surviving a head injury just wants to appear normal and emotional denial is a normal way to do that. To not have the conversation with people around you and to push aside memories and realistic action plans to cope with life is a normal thing. Anger and depression are the next phases in emotional recovery. "When you realize you are different and can't do things like you used to, you may become angry or depressed" (Johnson 2010). This is an accurate assessment of how a head injury survivor feels. When you are used to sustaining a way of life that is no longer possible, it is very hard to cope with. I had my injury when I was young, and it was hard to remain fit and stay in shape with the medication's weight gain side effect I went through. Finding my beauty and confidence from within was an adjustment that caused me to battle with depression.

Over time, I found ways to feel pretty, but I was unable to compete in pageants and model. Anger was an outlet emotion I expressed to the people I loved most. "People who are struggling to deal with vast changes produced by a head injury may get angry at the people around them . . . The sections of the brain that control those emotions have been injured." (Johnson 2010). My parents got most of my anger. I didn't always maintain self-control with my anger in circumstances involving my parents. My anger now can be triggered with my husband and marriage. It is something that I continually have to be mindful of and not let get out of control. The testing phase has its ups and downs. "[Survivors] test themselves to see their limits . . . I'll do things as I always did" (Johnson 2010). Over time, I tested my limits gradually. I tried different sports and activities and travel.

"They previously may have been an A or B student. They take a class and come out with a C or D, even though they may put in twice the effort of a C. For many people a C is a failure" (Johnson 2010). My case was completing my associate degree, pulling off straight As and excelling in statistics and physics. But once I was working through my bachelor's degree, I could not sustain those grades. I even had to repeat a class three times to pass and graduated with a B- average while having to withdraw a couple terms and come back when I was feeling better. The article says, "Many people with a head injury have a fatigue disorder. They know they get tired easily." Fatigue is something head injury survivors have to accept and plan for. According to Johnson, "They can only handle a limited number of hours of work or play. They've learned to make a consistent schedule and will stick to that schedule." I didn't work for a year after I graduated. I was able to work forty hours a week and then sixty-five hours a week for a year. I had trouble keeping up with housework, cleaning, and the rest of domestic life. Johnson added, "Often individuals in this phase use the 'old me' or the 'new me.'" Saying goodbye to the old me and hello to the new me "Often people who seem fine have more emotional problems than those with obvious disabilities" (Johnson 2010). This has been my experience. People sometimes expect more out of me than I can give. "In general people who tend to do well emotionally tend to have a very strong work ethic. They tend to believe it is important to contribute to society and to people around them. It's important to help people. They look outside of themselves to see what they can do to make the world around them better" (Johnson 2010). It takes a while to parse the survivor that is left after from the person that existed before the accident. At some point, it is very healthy to help others even if it is just an encouraging word to someone who has gone through a similar experience in the support group.

"Another factor in head injury is whether or not people freely admit to others that they have a head injury" (Johnson 2010). This was very emotional and difficult for me. To admit to someone outside of healthcare support workers, family, and friends that I had a head injury was out of the question. I did not want to be undermined or looked down upon and then have future uncomfortable interactions. In reality, people won't understand you unless they have the whole story. If they still treat you differently after they know, they are not worth being around anyways. Johnson says that "People who go to support groups often get a lot of positive feelings from being with other head injured people." Support groups have helped me. I think they are an important part of the recovery process.

Chapter 16

Returning to school after a head injury takes courage but is so important. It shapes your character, sharpens your brain, and forces social skills, confidence, and self-esteem. Sometimes, performance in grades will drop dramatically or maybe stay the same, but other parts of the brain will be harder to access. According to Johnson, "In each college, there will be a student services or special needs department…you need to have your doctor or neuropsychologist write a letter to document that you have a valid disability." I never took this opportunity in college. I made it work. In retrospect, this decision was born out of pride. The documented disability will allow things such as more time for tests, notes taken for you and other accommodations as needed. "Get with a partner or group and try to figure out what is the most important material to learn," Johnson recommended. This is an awesome strategy which doubles as social skill development. Some school strategies include, "test[ing] strategies and learn[ing] the material that was presented in class. Short term-memory will make it very hard to learn new material" (Johnson 2010). This is the most important drawback of a traumatic brain injury: to understand and work hard at overcoming. Study! Study! Study! Give yourself more time to learn things and ask questions and participate in class. "School has a fair amount of fatigue associated with it. With head injur[ies], people have limited energy" (Johnson 2010). Procrastination is a "no-no." Organizing and planning your time will serve you well. When you plan your day well, there will be adequate time for rest. "The problem is that socializing can get out of control if you don't spend time on your classes. You have to set your own limits and apply discipline. Don't get behind" (Johnson 2010). Friends should be set aside for a while (but not forgotten) in school until you get a rhythm of how to perform in school to the best of your ability. Friends should slowly be incorporated into your school life. Make sure to pick healthy relationships. Party friends may not understand you anymore. Find yourself before finding others.

Chapter 17

The road to recovery has many different stages. The first stage is right after the accident. From the chapter "When Will I Get Better," Johnson says that "The problem [is] that medical tests are not always the best predictors of long range outcome." Some MRI scans show damage, but the person may have a good recovery and others don't show damage on MRI scans and may have a slower recovery. "Psychologists use IQ tests to measure this (problem solving) ability" (Johnson 2010). I have not personally done this, so I am not sure that a test score can prove much. A person can gain better cognitive ability after a head injury through reading and studying. How a person performs in the school system whether K-12 or in college is a good indicator. According to Johnson, "Good performance in the educational system is a good predictor." This was helpful for me to stick with my goal in college. I persevered even when it was hard. Just because I did that, did not mean that my recovery process was equally as successful in other areas. "Some physicians say that recovery from head injury is 6 to 9 months" (Johnson 2010). I think that that time frame is the hardest part, and then from there, it is a year-long process to understand the injury better. After which, strategies for a return to normalcy may be implemented. "As a neuropsychologist, I look at complex thinking and subtle changes in behavior. I use psychological tests that look for changes in thinking and memory. Research on these tests indicate that for two years following a head injury, there is evidence of improving scores." (Johnson 2010). Thinking and behavior are important and should be constantly monitored. These capacities may improve and then worsen and improve and worsen. I have had to continually evaluate myself. "A lot of what a head injury program will do is improve [those] skills they can teach you [in terms of] coping [strategies]. This may include memory techniques and organizational strategies" (Johnson 2010). I have enjoyed my head injury programs and grown as a person. "You have to keep having faith. You have to keep working hard. Keep using the memory and organizational strategies," Johnson recommends. Head injuries take time to recover from. The process has ups and downs. Stay positive even though you may not have the physical or mental capability of before. You have a stronger character now, and you can help others. This process will help you meet and cope with other challenges in life better.

Chapter 18

I want to give my appreciation and thanks to the expertise of Glen Johnson in "Traumatic Brain Injury Survival Guide." All his work and scientific research adds an academic depth to my story and what I've experienced. Understanding how the frontal lobe works is extremely important as it is the biggest and most advanced part of the brain. Since this is where I was injured, this academic work makes sense of the wide array of problems I had. Common indicators of a head injury include becoming more easily tired and fatigued. This is the most prevalent side effect I have had over the years. I have found success through organizing my time, exercising, and getting adequate sleep. In the emotional stages of recovery, the frontal lobe area is affected. Through completing my associate and bachelor's degrees, I overcame these obstacles. I praise these as my most important accomplishments. When returning to school, doctors suggest writing a note to validate your disability. Since I was stubborn, I never did this, thinking I could get by the same as before. I would have succeeded even more in school with this added support. When will I get better is a question easier to ask than answer. Thinking and behavioral outcomes of a head injury are not predictable and must be constantly monitored. I had to train my brain.

I truly value my life before and after the accident. I grew up privileged with faith, family, and friends. If more traumatic brain injury survivors could write their stories, the world would better understand the life of an injured person. Our lives matter. Even if the "after" self can't accomplish what the "before" self could. It is important to move on and not feel sorry for oneself. Accomplish what is possible. After a traumatic brain injury, it is common to go to extremes. I could never do this or I can do that are common thoughts that create burn out. I have learned to live within realistic means. To strive for goals but give myself more time. People in my life who inspire and encourage me are my mom who loves horses and living on her own ranch and my mother-in-law who loves being a grandma and to cook. Inspiration wise, I may not be the same person I was before the injury, but I have modified my dreams and goals so I can still accomplish them within reasonable means. This includes finishing my degree although it took more time and modeling on the side in curvy sizes. The final dream I will tackle is to work in government administration one day. With hard work, dedication, and patience for myself, I can accomplish most things including writing this book.

www.ingramcontent.com/pod-product-compliance
Lightning Source LLC
Chambersburg PA
CBHW032052180726
48284CB00004B/1299